"Well, here they are now...

Three **fabulous** fleas!"

THE FLEAS WHO WOULDN'T SAY PLEASE

Lesley Sims

Illustrated by Siân Roberts

"It's Flynn, Fliss and Flossy on the

FLYING

TRAPEZE!"

"You're magic!" says Lady Spot, waving her hat.

Your flying's fantastic.

We know!

That evening, the fleas **WOW**.

They **dazzle**

and

shine.

Hurray!

They're the stars of the show!

After the show, they gather outside.
Hot chocolate is brought out in jugs.

Up strut the fleas.

They don't stop to say **PLEASE**...

...but just seize the three largest mugs.

Then they swan off
to bed.

Fame has gone
to their heads.

Those fleas really
are VERY rude.

Beetle agrees.
"They didn't say
PLEASE!"

Now everyone's
in a sad mood.

Bright and early,
the bugs are all working,
when Flynn bursts
right in and
shouts:

The ants march outside.
    "We can work on the grass."
    Then they slip on the mud and fall...

SPLAT!

Back in the Big Top, the fleas leap and dive.

R-R-RIP!

Oh no! Flossy misses a catch.

Look, there's a raggedy hole in her sleeve...

"Hey, Spider!" she calls.

Sew a patch!

"Not even a
thank you?"
thinks Spider.

Oh dear.

She's left
feeling sadder
than ever.

That night, the fleas are tremendous.
They **swing** and they **swoop** and they **sway**.

But just then,
TOOT!
TOOT!

The five clowns
drive in...

...AND CARRY THE
LADDER AWAY!

Now Bumble flies in.

"Earwigs!
Give it back."

And, all at once,
Fliss adds in, "**PLEASE?**"

The three fleas climb down
and take several bows.

The audience stands
up and cheers.

Hurray!

Next on, Lady Spot and a conjuring trick.

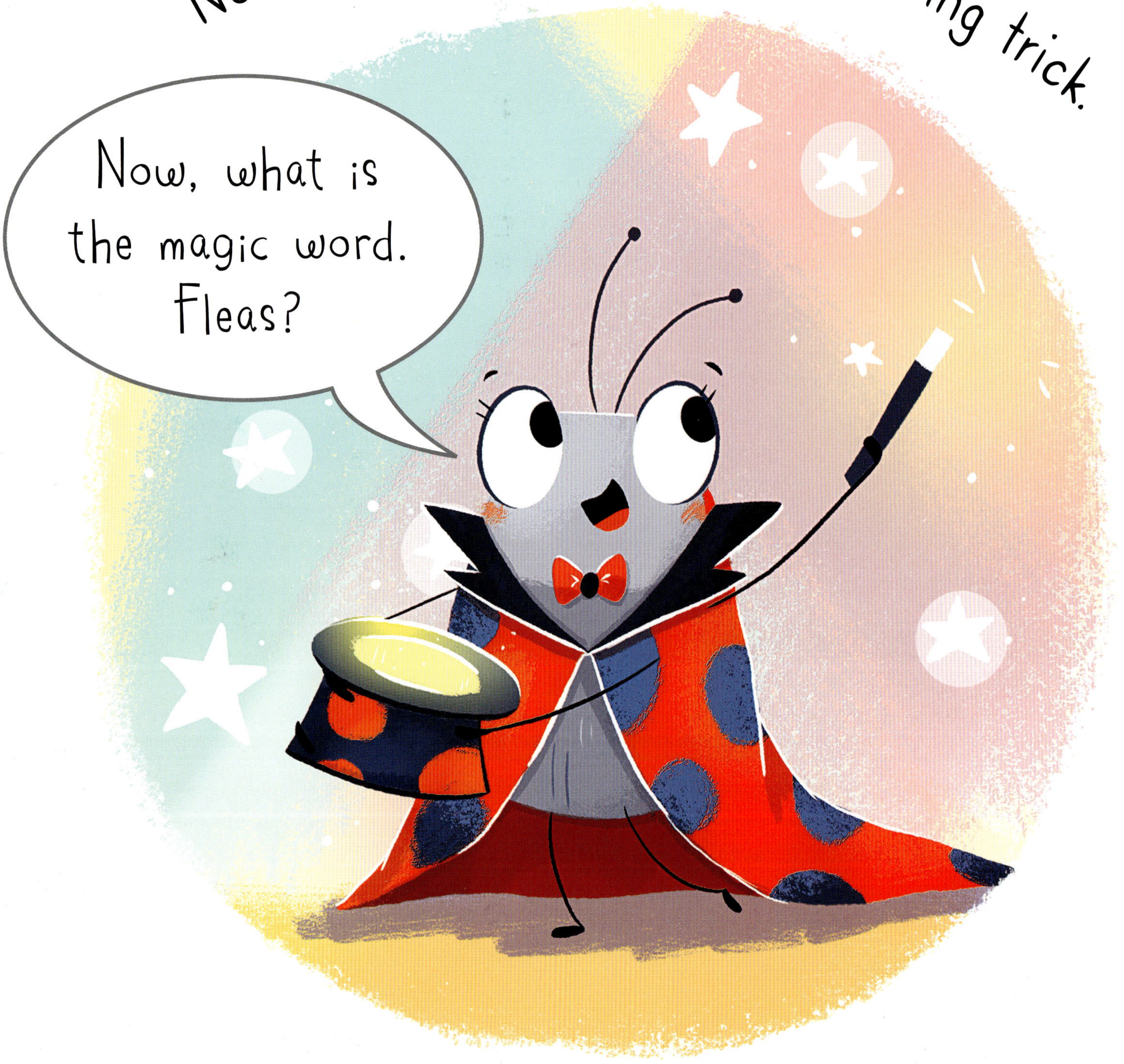

Designed by Laura Nelson Norris

This edition first published in 2024 by Usborne Publishing Limited, 83-85 Saffron Hill, London EC1N 8RT, United Kingdom.
usborne.com Copyright © 2024, 2023 Usborne Publishing Limited. The name Usborne and the Balloon logo are registered
trade marks of Usborne Publishing Limited. All rights reserved. No part of this publication may be reproduced, stored
in a retrieval system or transmitted in any form or by any means without prior permission of the publisher. UE.